The Day the Picture Man Came

by Faye Gibbons

Illustrated by Sherry Meidell

Boyds Mills Press

Boyds Mills Press, Inc.
A Highlights Company
815 Church Street
Honesdale, Pennsylvania 18431
Printed in China

Publisher Cataloging-in-Publication Data (U.S)

Gibbons, Faye.
The day the picture man came / by Faye Gibbons ; illustrated by Sherry Meidell. — 1st ed.
[32] p. : col. ill. ;   cm.
Summary: The arrival of a professional photographer brightens a young girl's day in this story
of an American farm family at the turn of the 20th century.
ISBN 1-56397-161-5
1. Farm life — Fiction. 2. Photographers — Fiction. I. Meidell, Sherry. II. Title.
[E] 21   CIP 2003
2002105794

First edition, 2003
The text of this book is set in 16-point Clearface Regular.

Visit our Web site at www.boydsmillspress.com

10 9 8 7 6 5 4 3 2 1

To Tim Howard and Bonnie Hibbert,
who love the Georgia mountains as I do
—F. G.

For Renae McBride
—S. M.

It was one of those days when I didn't like being Emily Howard one little bit.

I had plenty of reasons to be riled. First, my older sister Hazel fussed me out because I tried on her new bonnet, which almost made me look pretty. Before I could put the bonnet up, my older brother Bob's goat snatched it, and that got Mama down on me. Then my younger brother Wally's dogs chased my baby sister Jessie's cat through the house and spilled my jar of guaranteed freckle remover all over Papa's almanac.

To top everything, Mama sent us young'uns to the south pasture to pick blackberries, and, like usual, every stinging pest in the Georgia mountains was out to get me.

"I'm tired of berry picking," I said after the third deer fly bit me. "I wish something would happen."

Hazel sniffed and tossed her curls. "I think we've had enough going on around here today. Nothing more is going to happen."

She was dead wrong. A few minutes later, a brightly painted box of a wagon bounced around the far end of our pasture, headed for our house. It was pulled by a gray mule, and the driver wore flashy town clothes. We all dropped our berry buckets and tore out running.

Mama came out of the kitchen, wiping her hands on her apron, and Papa hurried from the barn. By the time the wagon pulled up by the hollow leaning oak at the edge of our front yard, they were waiting alongside us and the barking dogs.

"Cecil Bramlett here," the stranger said, jumping down from the wagon and holding out his hand to Mama and Papa. "And you'd be Mr. and Miz Howard, I reckon." He looked around at us sweaty kids in our ragged work clothes. "What handsome young'uns!"

Hazel tossed her curls and Mama and Papa smiled.

"A photograph of these children would be a treasure in years to come," said Mr. Bramlett, edging away from Bob's goat, Pete, who was sniffing at his shoelaces.

"Could Kitty be in it?" asked Jessie, holding her cat out for the man to see. The dogs growled and the cat hissed.

"King and Bo, too?" begged Wally, pushing the dogs forward.

"What about Pete?" demanded Bob.

Me and Hazel groaned. "Not the animals!" I said, but the picture
man nodded and Papa smiled at Mama.

"A family picture would be nice," he said.

"Everybody clean up and change clothes," ordered Mama,
heading for the house.

When we got back outside in our Sunday best, Mr. Bramlett had set two porch rockers in the yard. His three-legged camera stood in front of the old oak. Wally tugged the dogs into place while Bob tied an old straw hat on Pete.

"Pete faints when he gets scared," Bob bragged.

"I'll let you sit in the rockers," Mr. Bramlett told Mama and Papa. There was a tangle of young'uns and critters as the rest of us gathered around them.

"*Grr-r-r-r-r,*" said the dogs.

"*Ffffft!*" hissed the cat.

"*Ba-a-a-a!*" bleated the goat.

Hazel held her nose. "That old goat stinks!"

"So do the dogs," I said. "They've been rolling in something."

Mr. Bramlett kept smiling. "I'll put the pretty redhead here," he said and motioned for me.

"Me?" I said. "Pretty?"

"You stand right here," the picture man told Bob, placing him beside Mama. The goat suddenly reared up on the arm of Mama's rocker and grabbed her hat.

Mama shrieked and Pete fainted dead away.

I scooped up Mama's hat, and Mr. Bramlett hollered, "The goat goes next to Mr. Howard."

Bob and Wally dragged Pete over next to Papa's rocker. Jessie and I scrooched away from him.

Just as Mr. Bramlett went to his camera and threw a black cloth over it, Pete woke up and got to his feet. "Everybody smile," Mr. Bramlett said. Then Pete reached over to nibble Kitty's tail.

This was too much for Kitty. She leaped from Jessie's arms with a hiss and a screech.

"Row-row-row-row-row!" bellowed the dogs, taking off after her.

Pete keeled over.

"Meow-owww-owww!" yowled Kitty, shooting across the yard to the old oak. She threw herself into the mouth of the tree and scurried up and out of sight.

"Kitty!" screamed Jessie.

I hurried to get the dogs, but Bo was gone. I could hear him
scratching and clawing up inside the tree.

"Bo's climbing through the trunk!" bragged Wally.

Just then Kitty came out of an opening high as our house and
scampered out on a limb. Out came Bo moments later, still barking.
But all at once Bo looked down, saw how high he was, and tucked
in his tail. Hunkering down, he lifted his nose and howled,
"*Ar-oo-oo-oo-oo-oo-oo!*"

"Get the ladder," said Papa. Bob and Wally ran to fetch it.
Papa was soon propping the ladder against the tree. Up he went.
He climbed down with Bo across his shoulders.

"Now for the cat," he said. Just at that moment Kitty lost her balance and fell. She *whump-whump-whumped* from limb to limb and landed right on Mr. Bramlett.

The picture man threw up his hands and sat down in one of the rockers. He was sweating. I took him a dipper of water. "This is the same kind of luck I've been having all day," I told him. "Wish we could buy two pictures to pay you for your trouble."

Mr. Bramlett smiled. "You're smart," he said, and stood. "I'm going to make you folks a deal: two photographs for the price of one."

That's how we came to have two pictures hanging over the fireplace in our front room. One had just us Howards in it.

The other one had us with all the animals. Kitty was hissing,
the dogs were barking, and Pete looked ready to faint.

As for me, I looked like I felt mighty good about being Emily Howard—straight hair, freckles, and all!